# sous vide

## Meat

edited by Mary Dan Eades

photography by Mehosh Dziadzio

Paradox Press

# contents

# *introduction*

There is perhaps no corner of the larder where sous vide cooking makes a greater impact on the finished product than in the meat locker. No other cooking technique for meat—not the grill, the broiler, the sauté pan, or the rotisserie—can ensure such sublimely tender, reproducible, and succulent results. Only with sous vide cooking can a cut of meat be unfailingly cooked edge-to-edge to the preferred degree of doneness, whether that temperature is rare, medium-rare, medium, or more well-done. With no other method can the cook produce a perfectly rare or medium-rare and tender piece of flank steak or brisket. Medium-rare and tough are possible with other methods; overcooked and tender are possible with other methods—but not both. Yet, given a sufficient amount of time, the gentle and precise temperature of the sous vide water bath can effortlessly cook either of these cuts to perfection throughout, and have it fork tender to boot. And it can do it while the cook is doing something else.

Cooking an exceptional high-priced piece of meat doesn't take tremendous skill (although it can become transcendent with the right technique.) Just season a piece of dry-aged tenderloin of beef with a little salt and pepper and throw it on a hot barbee and you're likely to get something grand. But what of the lesser cuts? The family pack of New York strips or tri-tip steaks? The chuck roast, flank steak, and brisket?

Because meat makes up the central and usually most expensive sector on the family dinner plate, it's a real budget buster if it gets burned beyond recognition in a moment of distraction. And who doesn't have those moments? That's where the sous vide technique saves the day. Because sous vide allows the cook to dial in the perfect temperature for a given food and keep it precisely there throughout the process, the food cannot overcook, even if left for substantially longer than required. Once heated to temperature throughout, a piece of meat cooking sous vide can only become more tender if left in the water bath at its target temperature.

The road to perfection in sous vide cooking is all about the interplay of temperature, time, and texture. The first principle is that temperature dictates degree of doneness—the rare, medium-rare, medium, or more done spectrum—and time influences the final texture, meaning toughness or tenderness. The second is that perfection is relative. What one person views as a perfect medium-rare steak, for instance, may be seen as distinctly overcooked by someone else, and as undercooked by yet another. The beauty of this precise technique is that once you determine what's perfect to your taste, you can simply dial it in, degree by degree, time after time. In fact, once you become a veteran sous vide cook, you'll likely not talk of rare or medium-rare meat, but rather find yourself remarking, "I prefer my steaks at 134!" (That's Fahrenheit, of course. If you work from the Celsius scale, you'd prefer your steaks at 56.5!)

Costly, tender cuts of meat, such as beef or pork tenderloin, ribeye steaks, or lamb chops need only to be brought to the preferred degree of doneness throughout to be sublime. They are already tender, so they neither need nor benefit from a prolonged swim in the water bath, and in fact can become almost too tender if left for prolonged periods.

Tougher cuts of meat (flank steak, sirloin, brisket, chuck roast, stew meats, leg of lamb, spare ribs, pork shoulder), and very lean meats (grass-fed beef, bison, and game) need a sufficient amount of time in the water bath to reach their target temperature from edge to edge, based on their thickness. As soon as they've reached this target throughout, they can be safely eaten, but will be a challenge to chew. Tough cuts need additional time to become tender, typically 4 to 6 or even 8 hours of gentle simmering time. For some cuts, it may take as long as 30, 48 or even 72 hours for the meat to become fall-apart tender.

This book provides both a collection of kitchen-tested recipes for succulent and savory meats (beef, pork, and lamb) and all the basic instructions necessary for sous vide success on your very first try. Let's get to those basics now.

~ *Mary Dan Eades, Editor*

# the basics

Cooking sous vide (a French term meaning under vacuum) involves vacuum-sealing a given food—meat, fish, poultry, vegetables, fruit—in a food-grade pouch and submerging it in a temperature-controlled water bath for as long as it takes to bring the food to the desired temperature throughout. Food cooks gently and precisely and cannot overcook, since it can only reach the temperature of the water in the bath. Flavor and moisture that would normally escape into the air or drip into the pan stay locked in the food pouch, which produces the most flavorful, tender, and juicy food possible.

Chef George Pralus developed the technique in France about 40 years ago as a method for perfectly cooking, and minimizing the costly shrinkage, of foie gras. Chef Bruno Goussalt popularized the technique by introducing it in the first class cabin cuisine on Air France's international flights. Since then, it has become a favored cooking technique of great chefs around the globe and the secret weapon of chefs in competitions.

The introduction in 2009 of the SousVide Supreme,™ the first water oven designed for kitchen counter tops, made the technique practical for everyone, from the rank novice to the accomplished cook.

## How does sous vide cooking work?

Unlike traditional cooking methods, such as roasting, broiling, grilling, or sautéing, that use aggressively high temperatures to heat the air around the food, the sous vide technique relies on the superior ability of water to transfer heat to the food. Because the transfer of heat through water is many times faster than the transfer of heat

through air, removing all, or at least most, of the air from the cooking pouch—creating the vacuum seal—is important, as pockets of air between the pouch and the food can result in uneven cooking.

When cooking sous vide, the water bath temperature is set at precisely the desired target for doneness—for instance, 134°F (56.5°C) for perfectly medium rare beef. Foods cook gently for (at a minimum) long enough to allow the heat of the water to penetrate to the center of the food. How long that process takes has been carefully worked out mathematically for a wide variety of food types, and depends not as much on the weight of the food being cooked as on its thickness. For example, if it takes 40 minutes to bring a piece of steak that is one-inch thick to temperature, it might take two hours to bring a two-inch thick steak to that temperature. It is important, for food safety, to carefully adhere to the minimum cooking times and holding instructions.

## The simple steps of sous vide cooking

Season your food lightly with salt and pepper, or fresh or dried herbs and spices.

Seal the food in an appropriate sized food-grade cooking pouch. Use the vacuum-seal option for most foods, and the seal-only option or zip-closure cooking pouches for foods containing more than just a tablespoon of liquid.

Simmer the food at the desired temperature in the preheated water bath for at least the minimum recommended amount of time to ensure it is heated to the center. In most cases, you can leave the food in the water bath substantially longer without loss of quality.

Sear or sauce your food, if desired. All foods that have been cooked sous vide will be delicious straight from the pouch; but some benefit from a complementary sauce or a quick sear in a hot skillet, on a grill, or with a kitchen torch to impart the expected crisp, golden crust and savory flavor.

Serve!

## Tips for sous vide cooking

Every cooking technique has a learning curve, and sous vide is no different: success depends on learning the tricks of the trade. In traditional methods, that could be knowing when to add salt, or that it's important to add the dry ingredients to the wet when baking, or just when to pull the pudding from the heat as it thickens. While sous vide cooking is easy and undemanding, there are do's and don'ts. Here are some tips that will enhance your sous vide experience.

Fill the water oven with hot tap water before preheating to reduce the time it will take to reach the desired target temperature. Hot tap water generally exits the tap at 110° to 120°F (43° to 48°C), and will be much closer to most sous vide cooking temperatures than room temperature water.

Never overfill the cooking pouch. Use an appropriately sized pouch for the job at hand, or divide the food into smaller quantities and use multiple pouches.

Vacuum seal pieces of food—such as cut-up meat, fish, fruits, or vegetables—in a single layer for even cooking.

When using a suction vacuum sealer, use solid fats—such as butter, duck fat, bacon fat, and coconut oil—for seasoning, since they will not be pulled from the pouch by the sealer. Liquid oils or marinades leave a trail of oil or liquid along the sealing area, and generally result in an imperfect seal.

Freeze broths or liquids in small ice cube trays, and add to the pouch before vacuum sealing. They will melt and surround the food as it cooks in the water oven.

If using wine or other alcohol for an infusion or marinade, heat it first to evaporate the alcohol before adding it to the cooking pouch, since once sealed, the alcohol cannot evaporate and can impart a harsh flavor to the finished product.

Cook foods together that cook at, or near, the same temperatures.

## Food safety in sous vide cooking

As with all cooking methods, it is important to use clean, fresh ingredients and to work with clean hands and tools on clean surfaces. When cooking food sous vide for immediate consumption—what is termed *Cook-Serve*—the basic rules of food handling will suffice, because the food will remain hot in the machine until serving and may even get a final high-temperature sear.

Sometimes, especially when entertaining, it is helpful to employ a technique, used widely by restaurant chefs, called *Cook-Chill-Hold*. In this method, food is vacuum-sealed and cooked to completion in the water oven in advance, and then quick chilled in an ice water bath for long enough to return it to refrigerator temperature, and out of the so-called "danger zone." The danger zone is the temperature range between 40°F (5°C) and 130°F (54°C) where food-borne bacteria can grow most easily. Even though most of the potentially harmful bacteria will be killed by sous vide cooking, some can protect themselves from the heat by hibernating as dormant forms—called spores—that can blossom again given sufficient time and favorable temperatures.

To reduce the risk of food-borne illness when using the Cook-Chill-Hold method, follow these important guidelines:

• Quick chill the warm cooking pouches of food fully submerged in an ice water bath (half ice and half water) for long enough to ensure a quick drop back to refrigerated temperature. Generally this will be the same length as the minimum time required to bring the food to temperature. Add ice or freezer packs as needed.

• Immediately after chilling either refrigerate or freeze in the pouch.

• Hold refrigerated pouches of sous vide cooked food for no more than 48 hours; properly frozen food pouches should remain safe for up to one year.

• To ensure safety in holding, particularly with home refrigerators, be sure the refrigerator compartment maintains a temperature below 40°F (5°C), and that the freezer maintains a temperature below 0°F (-17°C).

beef

## 15
tri-tip with cilantro butter

## 16
Thai beef tenderloin

## 19
rainy day ribeye steaks

## 21
corned beef and cabbage

## 22
Korean barbecue short ribs

## 25
savory meatloaf

## 27
make ahead meatloaf

## 28
filet mignon with blackberry pear sauce

# tri-tip

*with cilantro butter*

1 pound (16 oz/.45 kg) tri-tip sirloin, about 2 inches (5 cm) thick, chilled

1 teaspoon (5 ml) kosher salt

1 teaspoon (5 ml) cracked pepper

2 teaspoons (10 ml) minced shallot

2 teaspoons (10 ml) lime juice

Vegetable oil, for oiling grill

*For the cilantro butter*

1 stick salted butter, softened

2 chipotle chilies in adobo, stemmed, seeded and minced

3 tablespoons (45 ml) chopped cilantro leaves

*Serves 4*

*Cooking time: 3 to 10 hours*

1. Fill and preheat the water oven to 134°F (56.5°C).

2. Season the tri-tip with the salt and pepper.

3. Transfer to a large (1 gallon/3.8 liter) food-grade cooking pouch and vacuum seal.

4. Submerge the pouch in the water oven and cook for at least 3 hours. (The meat will only become more and more tender the longer you leave it in the water oven, which you can do for as much as 10 hours.)

5. In a bowl, mix the shallots with the lime juice; let stand for 10 minutes.

6. Meanwhile, using a handheld mixer beat the butter, chipotle and cilantro at low speed until blended. Set aside.

7. Brush a skillet or grill grate with oil and preheat on high heat.

8. Remove the steak from the water; let stand in the pouch for 10 minutes, then remove the meat and pat it dry.

9. Sear the steak until browned and crusty, 30 seconds per side. Remove from the heat and let rest for 5 minutes.

10. Thinly slice the meat and top with the cilantro butter.

# _Thai_
# beef
# tenderloin

_Serves 4_
_Cooking time: 1 to 3 hours_

1. Fill and preheat the water oven to 134°F (56.5°C).

2. In a small saucepan, heat the vegetable oil and sauté the garlic over low heat until soft, about 3 minutes.

3. Remove the garlic pieces from the oil and drain them on paper towels. Reserve the oil; let it cool to room temperature.

4. Using a sharp paring knife, make ½-inch (1.3 cm) slits all over the tenderloin steaks and stuff the slits with the sautéed garlic pieces.

5. Fill a large (1 gallon/3.8 liter) zip-closure bag with the shallots, rosemary, thyme, lime zest, orange zest, fish sauce, soy sauce, dried chiles and the reserved garlic oil. Add the steaks and seal, turning to coat the meat with the marinade. Let stand at room temperature for 2 hours.

4 (8 ounce/227 g) filets of beef tenderloin, about 1½ inches (4 cm) thick

⅓ cup (75 ml) peanut oil

4 cloves garlic, peeled and sliced

2 shallots, peeled and thinly sliced

2 tablespoons (30 ml) chopped rosemary

2 tablespoons (30 ml) chopped thyme

1 lime, zest only

1 orange, zest only

2 tablespoons (30 ml) Asian fish sauce

⅓ cup (75 ml) low-sodium soy sauce

10 dried Thai chilies, coarsely chopped

1 tablespoon (15 ml) unsalted butter

1 tablespoon (15 ml) extra-virgin olive oil

6. Pour off marinade into a small saucepan and reserve for later use.

7. Vacuum seal the filets, 1 or 2 to a small (1 quart/.9 liter) zip-closure cooking pouch. Use Archimedes' Principle (page 61) to evacuate the air from the pouch, and zip closed. (If using standard vacuum-seal pouches, press as much air as possible out of the pouch with your hands, and seal only. Do not attempt to vacuum seal liquids with a suction vacuum sealer.)

8. Position the pouches in the slots of a pouch rack and submerge in the water oven, being sure the meat is entirely below the surface of the water.

9. Cook for at least 1 hour, but up to 3 hours. (Substantially longer cooking times for tender meats can result in a too-soft, mushy texture.)

10. When the cooking time has elapsed, remove the pouches from the water and allow the meat to cool for 10 minutes.

11. Meanwhile, in a small saucepan, bring the reserved marinade to a boil, reduce heat, and simmer to keep warm as a sauce to serve with the steaks.

12. In a skillet large enough to hold the filets comfortably (or working in batches to avoid overcrowding the pan) melt the butter in the olive oil and heat until nearly smoking.

13. Remove the steaks from the pouches and pat dry.

14. Sear the filets in the skillet 15-20 seconds per side, turning once, to form a brown crust.

15. Serve immediately and finish with sauce.

# steaks

Courtesy of Sally MacColl, SVKitchen.com

*Serves 2*
*Cooking time: 1½ to 3 hours*

2 boneless ribeye steaks, 1 to 1½ inches (2.5 cm to 3.8 cm) thick

2 tablespoons (30 ml) canola oil

2 cloves garlic, finely minced or pressed

2 teaspoons (10 ml) finely grated lemon zest

1 teaspoon (5 ml) truffle salt or more to taste

1 teaspoon (5 ml) ground fennel seed

1 teaspoon (5 ml) smoked paprika

1 teaspoon (5 ml) freshly ground black pepper

3 tablespoons (45 ml) butter, divided use (optional)

1. Fill and preheat the water oven to 134°F (56.5°C).

2. Trim the steaks of excess outside fat; rinse them and pat dry.

3. In a small bowl, combine the seasonings and mix well.

4. Rub one side of the steaks with half the oil and sprinkle half the seasoning mixture over them. Flip steaks over and repeat.

5. Put each steak into a small (1 quart/.9 liter) food-grade cooking pouch and vacuum seal. (At this point, the steaks can be refrigerated for up to a day in advance of cooking.)

6. Submerge the pouches in the water oven and cook the steaks for a minimum of 90 minutes or up to 3 hours. (Substantially longer cooking times can result in a too-soft texture.)

7. Remove the steaks from the pouches and drain the accumulated juices into a small

bowl or ramekin; set aside.

8. Lightly pat the steaks with paper towels to dry the surface.

9. Heat a skillet large enough to hold both steaks over medium-high heat until the pan is very hot. If using butter, add 2 tablespoons (30 ml) to the hot pan and immediately add the steaks. Sear the meat for 1 minute, then turn and sear the other side for 30 seconds. Immediately transfer the steaks to warm serving plates.

10. For the optional pan sauce, add the reserved cooking juices to the skillet and cook until reduced by half, about 1 minute.

11. Remove the pan from the heat and whisk in the remaining 1 tablespoon (15 ml) of butter.

12. Pour the sauce over the steaks and serve immediately.

# corned
# beef

*and cabbage*

4 pounds (1.81 kg) of corned beef

6 slices of bacon, cut into ½-inch (1.3 cm) strips

1 head of cabbage, cut into 1-inch (3 cm) strips

2 cups (10 oz/473 ml) chicken stock

½ cup (4 fl oz/120 ml) champagne vinegar

*Serves 6 to 8*
*Cooking time: 48 hours*

1. Fill and preheat the water oven to 134°F (56.5°C).

2. Put the corned beef into a food-grade cooking pouch and vacuum seal.

3. Submerge the pouch in the water oven and cook for 48 hours

4. About 45 minutes before you are ready to serve the meal, prepare the cabbage.

5. In a skillet, over medium heat, cook the bacon pieces until they are crisp and the fat is rendered. Pour off all but 1-2 tablespoons (15 to 30 ml) of the bacon fat.

6. Add the cabbage strips to the skillet, raise the heat to medium-high, and cook for about 5 minutes.

7. Add the chicken stock and the vinegar to the pan and continue to cook the cabbage in the liquid until tender.

8. When the cabbage is almost tender, remove the corned beef from the water bath and the cooking pouch.

9. To serve, slice the corned beef into ½- to ¾-inch (1.3 to 2 cm) slices and serve atop the cabbage.

# Korean barbecue short ribs

6 pounds (2.72 kg) beef short ribs, cut crosswise into twelve 2½-inch (6.4 cm) squares (ask your butcher to cut the ribs for you)

Peanut oil

*For the marinade*

1 cup (240 ml) soy sauce*

4 large cloves garlic, peeled and chopped or (already prepared minced)

2 tablespoons (30 ml) finely grated peeled fresh ginger or (already prepared minced)

4 scallions, thinly sliced

¼ cup (1.8 oz/50 g) sugar

2 tablespoons (30 ml) sesame oil

Freshly ground black pepper

*Serves 6*
*Cooking time: 48 hours*

*Make the marinade*

1. In a medium bowl, whisk together the soy sauce, garlic, ginger, scallions, sugar, and sesame oil.

2. Season with black pepper.

3. Use marinade immediately or refrigerate in a tightly sealed container for up to 2 days.

*Marinate the short ribs*

1. Place the ribs in a single layer in a large glass baking dish. Pour about three-quarters of the marinade over the ribs, and turn them to coat evenly. Reserve the remaining marinade for serving.

2. Cover the dish and refrigerate; allow the ribs to marinate for at least 2 hours or up to 8 hours.

*\*Note: Not all soy sauces are the same. Some are saltier, others sweet and thick. For the best results with this marinade, choose a dark Japanese or Korean soy sauce.*

*Cook the short ribs*

1. Fill and preheat the water oven to 132°F (55.5°C).

2. Remove the ribs from the marinade and blot them with a damp paper towel.

3. Put the ribs into food-grade cooking pouches in a single layer (4 rib squares per 1 quart/.9 liter pouch) and vacuum seal.

4. Using a pouch rack, arrange the cooking pouches side by side, being sure there is space between the pouches and that all meat is fully submerged below the surface of the water.

5. Cook for 48 hours.

6. When ready to finish the ribs for serving, oil the grate of a gas or charcoal grill and preheat to high heat.

7. Remove the ribs from the vacuum pouches, pat them dry, and sear them on the grill, meaty side down until browned, approximately 1 minute per side. (Alternately, sear in a very hot sauté pan with a little bit of peanut oil until browned, approximately 1 minute per side.) Set ribs aside to rest for 5 minutes.

8. Serve with a side of reserved marinade for dipping.

# *savory*
# meatloaf

*Serves 6*
*Cooking time: 3 to 6 hours*

1. Preheat the water oven to 150°F (65°C).

2. Put the chili sauce, pepper jelly, chipotle peppers and adobo sauce in the work bowl of a food processor or a blender jar and process until smooth to make the chipotle glaze. Set aside.

3. In a large skillet over medium high heat, add the olive oil and, when hot, sauté the onion, bell pepper and poblano until they are very soft, 6 to 8 minutes.

4. Add the garlic, Southwest Seasoning, salt and oregano and cook for 2 more minutes. Remove skillet from the heat and allow the vegetable mixture to cool slightly.

1 cup (4 oz/240 g) sweet chili sauce

2 tablespoons (30 ml) pepper jelly

2 chipotle peppers in adobo sauce, plus 1 tablespoon (15 ml) adobo sauce

2 tablespoons (30 ml) olive oil

1 large onion, peeled and chopped

1 large red bell pepper, stemmed, seeded and finely chopped

1 poblano pepper, stemmed, seeded and finely chopped

2 tablespoons (30 ml) minced garlic

1½ teaspoons (7.5 ml) Southwest Seasoning

1 teaspoon (5 ml) salt

1 teaspoon (5 ml) dried oregano or Mexican oregano (optional)

1 pound (16 oz/0.45 kg) ground sirloin

1 pound (16 oz/0.45 kg) fresh Italian sausage, medium or hot

2 eggs, beaten

½ cup (4 fl oz/125 ml) heavy cream

Additional spicy adobo sauce (optional)

5. In a large mixing bowl, combine the cooled vegetable mixture, sirloin, sausage, eggs, heavy cream, and 1 tablespoon of the glaze, and mix, gently but thoroughly, until well blended. Reserve the remaining glaze for finishing.

6. Transfer the meat mixture to a small (1 quart/.9 liter) food-grade cooking pouch, pushing it evenly across the bottom of the pouch to create a loaf approximately 2½ to 3 inches (6.5 to 7.5 cm) thick. Use the side of your hand on the outside of the pouch to press the meat into a tight loaf at the bottom. Vacuum seal the pouch.

7. Submerge the pouch in the water oven and cook for at least 3 hours, but up to 6 hours should not affect the texture.

8. When ready to serve, remove the meatloaf from the pouch, pat dry with a paper towel, top with the reserved chipotle glaze and sear under the broiler, set on high, for 5 minutes to brown the surface. Slice and enjoy!

# meatloaf

*Serves 6*
*Cooking time: 4 to 8 hours*

1. Assemble the ingredients for the Savory Meatloaf on page 25 and complete steps 3 through 6 of the recipe.

2. Transfer the meat mixture to a 1 quart/.9 liter food-grade cooking pouch that has been placed within a 6 x 9-inch (15 cm x 23 cm ) loaf pan, and smooth the meat to form a loaf.

3. Spoon about ⅔ of the chipotle glaze evenly over the top of the meatloaf, reserve the remaining sauce in a food-grade cooking pouch, seal, and freeze.

4. Seal the meatloaf pouch, and freeze.

*Cook the meatloaf*

1. Fill and preheat the water oven to 150°F (65°C).

2. Remove the frozen meatloaf cooking pouch from the loaf pan, open the pouch and vacuum seal.

3. Place the pouch in the water bath and cook for at least 4 hours or up to 8 hours.

4. If using the reserved frozen adobo sauce, add the pouch to the water bath 1 hour before you will serve the meal.

5. When ready to serve, remove the meatloaf from the pouch, slice, and top with the additional adobo sauce, if desired.

# filet mignon

with blackberry pear sauce

2 filet mignon steaks, about 2 inches (5 cm) thick

1 fresh pear, whatever type is in season in your area

½ cup (4 fl oz/120 ml) high-quality balsamic vinegar

2 tablespoons (30 ml) blackberry jam

1 tablespoon (15 ml) flaky sea salt

1 teaspoon (15 ml) freshly ground black pepper

2 tablespoons (60 ml) butter

Courtesy of Stephanie Stiavetti
of Wasabimon.com

*Serves 2*
*Cooking time: 1 to 4 hours*

1. Fill and preheat the water oven to 134°F (56.5°C) for medium-rare; 140°F (60°C) for medium; or 150°F (65.5°C) for medium-well.

2. Pat steaks dry and set aside.

3. Peel the pear, then cut it in half, remove the seeds, and purée in a food processor until smooth.

4. In a small saucepan over a medium heat, combine the balsamic vinegar, blackberry jam and 2 tablespoons of the pear puree. Stirring occasionally, heat the mixture until it has thickened substantially, about 15 minutes.

5. Once the sauce has adequately reduced, remove it from the heat.

6. Give the steaks a final pat down to remove any remaining moisture. Sprinkle both sides with salt and pepper, and drop a tablespoon-full of the reduction onto each

steak, giving it a little swirl to cover the surface. Reserve the remainder of the reduction sauce.

7. Put both steaks into a small (1 quart/.9 liter) food-grade cooking pouch and vacuum seal.

8. Put the pouch into the water bath, making sure the meat is fully submerged to ensure even cooking.

9. Cook for 1 hour, and no longer than 4 hours. (Longer cooking times can result in a too-soft texture.)

10. When steaks have just about finished cooking, reheat the reserved blackberry pear reduction sauce over a medium-low flame. Swirl in the butter and leave the sauce simmering over a very low heat once the butter is melted. Occasionally stir with a spatula or wooden spoon to keep from burning.

11. Meanwhile, heat a small skillet over medium-high heat for a minute or two.

12. Remove the steaks from the cooking pouch, pat them dry, and sear each side for 30 seconds or so in the hot skillet.

13. Serve immediately, topped with the blackberry pear sauce.

*pork*

## 33
barbecue ribs and sweet corn tomalito

## 35
sweet corn tomalito

## 36
pork peperonata with brown rice

## 39
sous vide tamales

## 43
stuffed pork tenderloin

## 45
Jamaican jerk pork

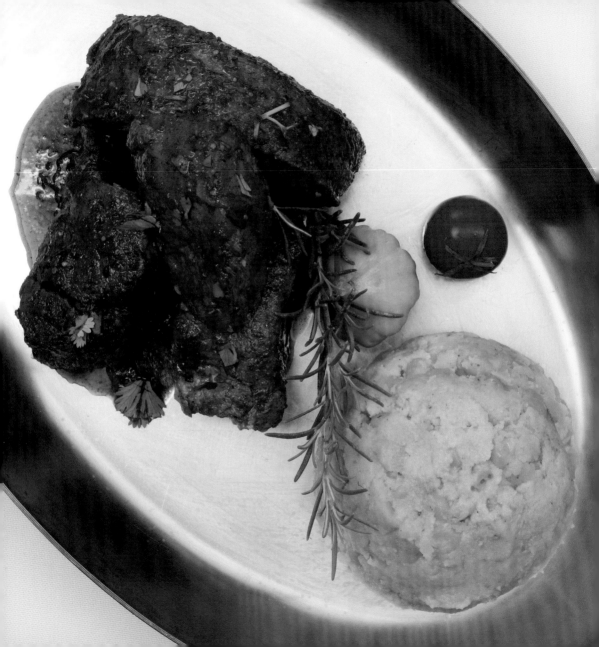

# barbecue ribs

*and sweet corn*
*tomalito*

From the kitchen of
Katherine Emmenegger, C.C.C.
great-news.com

*Serves 4*
*Cooking time: 8 to 12 hours*

1. Fill and preheat the water oven to
160°–176°F (71°–80°C).

2. Season the pork ribs with salt,
pepper, and chili powder.

3. In a skillet, over high heat, heat
the oil and sear the pork to brown
on each side, about 30 seconds.
Set aside the pork ribs.

1 teaspoon (5 ml) salt

½ teaspoon (2.5 ml) black pepper

1 tablespoon (15 ml) chile powder

2 tablespoons (30 ml) vegetable oil

2 pounds (32 0z/0.91 kg) boneless
country style pork ribs, rinsed and
patted dry with a paper towel

1 yellow onion, peeled and
julienned

1 red bell pepper, washed, cored,
and julienned

3 garlic cloves, peeled and minced

1 (12 oz/340 g) bottle Heinz
chili sauce

½ cup (4 fl oz/120 ml) water

3 tablespoons (45 ml) red wine
vinegar

1 teaspoon (5 ml) Worcestershire
sauce

2 teaspoons (10 ml) Dijon mustard

2 teaspoons (10 ml) chili powder

½ teaspoon (2.5 ml) celery seed

3 tablespoons (45 ml) brown sugar

Salt and pepper to taste

4. In the same pan, sauté the onions, peppers, and garlic until lightly browned; about
1 to 2 minutes.

5. Add all remaining ingredients and bring to a simmer. Pour the sauce over the pork.

6. Transfer the ribs into a large (1 gallon/3.8 liter) zip-closure cooking pouch. Use Archimedes' Principle (page 61) to evacuate the air from the pouch, and zip closed. (If using standard vacuum-seal pouches, press as much air as possible out of the pouch with your hands, and seal only. Do not attempt to vacuum seal liquids with a suction vacuum sealer.)

7. Submerge the pouch in the water oven and cook for 8 to 12 hours. The food must be submerged completely for even cooking.

8. When ready, remove ribs from the pouch and transfer to a warm plate. Serve with the Sweet Corn Tomalito.

# *sweet corn*
# tomalito

From the kitchen of
Katherine Emmenegger, C.C.C.
great-news.com

*Serves 4*
*Cooking time: 2 to 8 hours*

½ cup (2.5 oz/125 g) cornmeal

¼ cup (1.3 oz/37.5 g) masa harina

1 teaspoon (5 ml) baking powder

½ teaspoon (2.5 ml) salt

1 cup (8 oz/230 g) fresh corn cut from the cob (about 2 medium ears) or frozen whole-kernel corn, thawed

½ cup (4 fl oz/120 ml) whole milk

5 tablespoons (75 ml) softened, unsalted butter or vegetable shortening

⅓ cup (2.4 oz/67 g) granulated sugar

1. Fill and preheat the water oven to 176°F (80°C).

2. In a bowl, combine all ingredients.

3. Put the corn mixture into a large (1 gallon/3.8 liter) zip-closure cooking pouch. Use Archimedes' Principle (page 61) to evacuate the air from the pouch, and zip closed. (If using standard vacuum-seal pouches, press as much air as possible out of the pouch with your hands, and seal only. Do not attempt to vacuum seal liquids with a suction vacuum sealer.)

4. Submerge the pouch in the water bath and cook for 2 to 8 hours. It must be submerged completely to ensure even cooking.

5. When ready, remove the tomalito from the water bath, open the pouch, and serve with barbecue pork ribs or your favorite barbecued meat or poultry.

# pork
# peperonata
## with brown
## rice

2 tablespoons (30 ml) grapeseed oil

4 bone-in center cut pork chops, about ¾ inches (1.9 cm) thick

Salt and pepper, to taste

1 small yellow onion, peeled and julienned

1 green bell pepper, washed, cored, and julienned

1 tablespoon (15 ml) minced garlic

2 cups (16 fl oz/473 ml) vegetable or chicken broth

½ cup (2 oz/120 ml) tomato puree

1 cup (7 oz/207 g) long grain brown rice

2 tablespoons (30 ml) butter

4 sprigs fresh rosemary

From the kitchen of
Katherine Emmenegger, C.C.C.
great-news.com

*Serves 4*
*Cooking time: 4 to 8 hours*

1. Fill and preheat the water oven to 140°F (60°C).

2. Season the pork chops with salt and pepper.

3. In a skillet over high heat, quickly sear the pork chops in the oil to brown, about 30 seconds each side.

4. In the same pan, sauté the onions, peppers, and garlic until lightly browned; about 1 to 2 minutes.

5. Add the broth, tomato puree, and the rice and stir to combine. Remove from the heat.

6. Put the chops in small (1 quart/.9 liter) zip-closure cooking pouches in a single layer,

two chops per pouch.

7. Divide the rice mixture between the pouches and add 1 tablespoon (15 ml) of butter and 2 sprigs of rosemary to each pouch.

8. Use Archimedes' Principle (page 61) to evacuate the air from the pouch, and zip closed. (If using standard vacuum-seal pouches, press as much air as possible out of the pouch with your hands, and seal only. Do not attempt to vacuum seal liquids with a suction vacuum sealer.)

9. Put the pouches into the water bath, making sure the food is fully submerged to ensure even cooking.

10. Cook for 4 to 8 hours.

11. When ready to serve, transfer the pouches to a tray. Open the pouches and remove the rosemary sprigs. Spoon the rice onto serving dishes, top each with a pork chop, and enjoy.

# tamales

From the kitchen of
Katherine Emmenegger, C.C.C.
great-news.com

*Makes 36 tamales*
*Cooking time: 8 to 10 hours for the filling,*
*plus 2 to 6 hours for the tamales*

1. Fill and preheat the water oven to
134°F (56.5°C).

2. Rinse the pork, pat it dry, and cut
the meat into approximately ¼-pound
(4 oz/113 g) chunks.

3. Season the pork with the salt, pepper,
and chili powder to taste.

4. Divide the pork, onions, garlic, and
broth evenly between two large
(1 gallon/3.8 liter) zip-closure cooking
pouches. Use Archimedes' Principle
(page 61) to evacuate the air from the
pouch, and zip closed. (If using standard
vacuum-seal pouches, press as much

*For the spicy pork filling*

4 pounds (1.81 kg) pork shoulder,
bone in, (Boston Butt)

Salt, pepper, and chili powder,
to taste

2 large yellow onions, peeled and
julienned

4 garlic cloves, peeled and crushed

2 cups (16 fl oz/473 ml) vegetable
broth

*For the red sauce*

2 tablespoons (30 ml) vegetable oil

1 large yellow onion, peeled and
diced small

2 garlic cloves, peeled and minced

1 can (28 oz/828 g) tomato puree

2 tablespoons (30 ml) ground
cumin or to taste

3 tablespoons (45 ml) ancho chile
powder or to taste

1 tablespoon (15 ml) dried oregano,
crumbled, or to taste

Salt and cayenne pepper, to taste

*For the masa*

4 cups (20 oz/600 g) packed dry
masa mix

1 tablespoon (15 ml) baking
powder, best if fresh

2 teaspoons (10 ml) salt

(continued on next page)

air as possible out of the pouch with your hands, and seal only. Do not attempt to vacuum seal liquids with a suction vacuum sealer.)

5. Put the pouches into the water bath, making sure the pouches are completely submerged to ensure even cooking.

6. Cook for 8 to 10 hours.

7. When ready, remove the pork from the pouches to a sheet tray to cool.

8. Remove any visible fat and shred the meat.

4 cups (32 fl oz/946 ml)) beef, chicken, or vegetable broth

1⅓ cups (9.3 oz/264 g) lard or vegetable shortening

*For the tamales*

2 bags of corn husks

*Make the red sauce*

1. In a saucepan, over medium heat, heat the oil and sauté the onions and garlic for 3 to 4 minutes.

2. Add the tomato puree, cumin, ancho chile powder, and oregano.

3. Simmer for 20 minutes.

4. Adjust the seasonings with salt and cayenne pepper and let cool.

5. Mix the red sauce with the shredded meat, and follow the directions for tamale preparation and cooking. The sauce may be stored in the refrigerator in an airtight container for up to 3 days, if not to be used right away.

*Make the masa*

1. In a deep bowl, combine the masa, baking powder, and salt, and mix well.

2. Pour the broth into the masa a little at a time, working it in with your fingers.

3. In a large bowl, use an electric mixer, fitted with the paddle attachment if you have it, to whip the lard or shortening until fluffy; add the masa and combine until just mixed.

*Assemble and cook the tamales*

1. Fill and preheat the water oven to 176°F (80°C).

2. Soak the corn husks in hot water for 1 hour.

3. Remove the silk.

4. Rinse the husks and drain well.

5. Using the largest husks, lay them flat on a plate or work surface with the smooth side up and the narrow end facing you.

6. Scoop 3 tablespoons (45 ml) of the masa onto a husk; lay a piece of plastic wrap over the masa and press with your palm to flatten. Remove the plastic wrap and use for the remaining tamales.

7. Put about 2 to 3 tablespoons (30 to 45 ml) of pork filling down the center of the masa, bring the long sides of the husk together to encase the filling in masa, fold the bottom of the husk up, and roll the husk from the bottom, but not too tightly.

8. Arrange the rolled tamales evenly in two large (1 gallon/3.8 liter) zip-closure cooking pouches, in no more than two layers.

9. Use Archimedes' Principle (page 61) to evacuate the air from the pouches, and zip closed. (Or press the air from a standard, food-grade vacuum pouch and seal only.)

10. Submerge the pouches in the water bath and cook for 2 to 6 hours. The food must be submerged completely to ensure even cooking.

11. Carefully open the pouches and remove the tamales. The tamales are done when the masa pulls cleanly away from the husk. The tamale should be soft, yet firm and not mushy.

12. Serve with accompaniments such as salsas, sour cream, and cilantro.

*stuffed pork*

# tenderloin

From the kitchen of
Katherine Emmenegger, C.C.C.
great-news.com

*Serves 6*
*Cooking time: 6 to 8 hours*

2 tablespoons (30 ml) olive oil

½ cup (1.5 oz/43 g) diced leeks,
white part only, washed well

3 shallots, peeled and diced

2 large garlic cloves, peeled
and minced

1 tablespoon (15 ml) minced fresh
thyme leaves

¼ cup (.7 oz/19 g) minced fresh
Italian parsley leaves

2 cups (3 oz/90 g) panko bread
crumbs

Salt and pepper to taste

2 (1 lb/.45 kg each) pork tenderloins

1. Fill and preheat the water oven to
140°F (60°C).

2. In a skillet, over medium high heat, heat the oil and sauté the leek, shallots, and
garlic until softened, about 5 minutes.

3. Add the thyme and parsley and sauté 2 minutes more.

4. Stir in the bread crumbs, salt, and pepper, and set aside to cool completely.

5. Trim the fat and remove the silver skin from the tenderloins, butterfly them, and
pound out to an even thickness.

6. Season the pork with the salt and pepper on either side.

7. Spread the surfaces of the loins with the stuffing and roll in jelly-roll fashion.

8. Truss the pork with cotton kitchen twine.

9. Put each stuffed tenderloin into a food-grade cooking pouch and vacuum seal.

10. Submerge the food pouches in the water bath.

11. Cook at least 6 hours, but up to 8 hours will not affect the texture.

12. Remove the meat from the pouches, pat dry, and let stand for 5 minutes.

13. Sear for one minute per side over high heat on the grill or in a skillet.

14. Remove the kitchen twine, slice, and serve.

# Jamaican
# jerk pork

*Serves 6 to 8*
*Cooking time: 24 hours*

1. Fill and preheat the water oven to 155°F (68°C).

2. Make the Jamaican jerk rub by combining all ingredients in a bowl.

3. Season the pork liberally on all sides with the Jamaican jerk rub. (Reserve the remaining jerk rub in a zip closure bag for later use.)

4. Put the roast into a large (1gallon/3.8 liter) food-grade cooking pouch and vacuum seal.

3 pounds (48 oz/1.36 kg) pork roast (Boston butt roast or picnic roast)

½ cup (1.5 oz/43 g) onion chopped

*For the Jamaican jerk rub*

1 tablespoon (15 ml) onion flakes

1 tablespoon (15 ml) onion powder

1 tablespoon (15 ml) garlic powder

2 teaspoons (10 ml) ground thyme

2 teaspoons (10 ml) sugar

2 teaspoons (10 ml) dried chives

2 teaspoons (10 ml) sea salt

1 teaspoon (5 ml) ground allspice

1 teaspoon (5 ml) coarse black Pepper

½ teaspoon (2.5 ml) cayenne

½ teaspoon (2.5 ml) chipotle chili powder

¼ teaspoon (1.25 ml) ground nutmeg

¼ teaspoon (1.25 ml) ground cinnamon

5. Submerge the food pouch in the water bath completely, and cook for 24 hours.

6. When ready to serve, remove the roast from the pouch and pat it dry.

7. In a hot skillet over high heat, quickly sear the roast in vegetable oil to brown the surface before shredding.

8. Let the meat cool slightly and using two forks, shred the roast.

9. Serve the meat on a toasted bun or over cooked rice with black beans.

*lamb*

*49*

Mediterranean lamb shanks

*50*

rack of lamb with mint sauce

*52*

Irish lamb stew

*55*

Greek lamb pita wraps

*57*

shepherd's pie

# Mediterranean
## lamb shanks

4 lamb shanks

1 medium yellow onion, peeled and diced medium

2 large garlic cloves, peeled and minced

1 can (28 ounces/794 g) diced tomatoes

½ cup (4 oz/120 ml) dry red wine

2 tablespoons (2 ml) all-purpose flour

2 teaspoons (10 ml) dry oregano

Salt and pepper, to taste

½ cup (3.5 oz/99 g) orzo pasta

Fresh rosemary, for garnish

From the kitchen of
Katherine Emmenegger, C.C.C.
great-news.com

*Serves 4*
*Cooking time: 12 to 30 hours*

1. Fill and preheat the water oven to 160–176°F (71–80°C).

2. Caramelize the surface of the lamb shanks in a 400°F (204°C) oven, turning regularly, or brown with a kitchen torch.

3. In a bowl, combine the wine and flour and mix to a smooth consistency.

4. Divide ingredients evenly between two large (1 gallon/3.8 liter) zip-closure cooking pouches, use Archimedes' principle (page 61) to evacuate the air, and zip closed. (Or press the air from a standard, food-grade vacuum pouch and seal only.)

5. Submerge the pouches in the water oven, and cook for 12 to 30 hours. The food must be submerged completely to ensure even cooking.

6. During the last hour of cooking, open the pouches, add the orzo pasta to each pouch, reseal, and return to the water bath.

7. When ready, remove the pouches, carefully open them, and arrange the shanks and orzo on serving plates.

8. Garnish with a sprig of rosemary.

# rack of lamb

*with mint sauce*

2 lamb racks, Frenched
(or 12 meaty t-bone lamb chops)

Salt and pepper to taste

*For the herbed butter*

2 tablespoons (30 ml) butter

1 clove garlic, peeled and pressed

½ teaspoon (2.5 ml) onion powder

1 teaspoon (5 ml) fresh rosemary
leaves, minced

1 tablespoon (15 ml) grated
Parmesan

*For the mint sauce*

2 tablespoons (30 ml) fresh mint
leaves, minced

⅓ cup (2.6 fl oz/77 ml) apple cider
or red wine vinegar

2 teaspoons (10 ml) sugar
(or 1 packet sweetener)

*Serves 4*
*Cooking time: 1½ to 4 hours*

1. Fill and preheat the water oven
to 134°F (56.5°C).

2. Sprinkle both sides of the racks
or chops liberally with salt and pepper.

3. Put each lamb rack (or 3 to 4 chops)
into a small (1 quart/.9 liter) food-grade cooking pouch and vacuum seal.

4. Submerge the food pouches in the water bath and cook for at least 1½ hours (but
up to 4 hours will not affect the texture of the meat.)

*Make the mint sauce*

1. Whisk all ingredients together in a small bowl

2. Let the sauce sit at room temperature for 15 to 20 minutes to allow flavors to blend.

*Finish the lamb*

1. At the end of the lamb's cooking time, melt the butter and combine with all remain-

ing herbed butter ingredients.

2. When ready to serve, remove the lamb from the pouches, pat the surface dry, and brush all over with the herbed butter mixture.

3. Sear the lamb quickly on one side in a hot skillet or for about 3 minutes under the broiler. (Sear the rack meaty side down in the skillet or meaty side up under the broiler.)

4. Slice the rack into chops and top with Fresh Mint Sauce, if desired.

# Irish
# lamb stew

*Serves 6*
*Cooking time: 8 to 10 hours*

1. Fill and preheat the water oven to 185°F (80°C).

2. Put 2 tablespoons (60 ml) of the olive oil into a skillet over medium high heat.

3. When hot, add the stew meat and sear quickly on all sides to brown the surface; remove meat to a large bowl and set aside.

4. Add the remaining olive oil and the butter to the skillet and heat until the butter has melted.

4 tablespoons (60 ml) extra virgin olive oil, divided use

2 pounds (0.91 kg) lamb stew meat, cut into 1-inch (2.5 cm) chunks

2 tablespoons (30 ml) unsalted butter

4 tablespoons (60 ml) flour

2 tablespoons (30 ml) minced garlic

1 quart (32 fl oz/946 ml) beef stock

1½ pounds (24 oz/710 g) baby Yukon gold or red new potatoes, halved

1 pound (16 oz/473 g) baby carrots (about one bag)

1 cup (4 oz/110 g) frozen or fresh green peas

2 cans (28 oz/828 g) stewed tomatoes

4 sprigs fresh thyme

1 sprigs fresh rosemary

2 whole sprigs fresh mint

Sour cream or crème Fraiche for garnish

5. Add the garlic and cook briefly, but do not brown.

6. Sprinkle in the flour to make a roux, whisking continuously for about 2 minutes.

7. Add 2 to 3 cups (16 to 24 fl oz/473 ml to 710 ml) of the beef stock and continue

to whisk until the pan liquids reach the thickness you prefer for the stew. Add more or less liquid to your liking.

8. Add all vegetables and herbs to the stew meat in the bowl and mix well.

9. Divide all ingredients, including the pan liquid, evenly between two large (1 gallon/ 3.8 liter) zip-closure cooking pouches. Use Archimedes' Principle (page 61) to evacuate the air from the pouch, and zip closed. (If using standard vacuum-seal pouches, press as much air as possible out of the pouch with your hands, and seal only. Do not attempt to vacuum seal liquids with a suction vacuum sealer.)

10. Put the food pouches into the water oven, and cook for 8 to 10 hours. The food must be submerged completely to ensure even cooking.

11. When ready, remove the stew from pouches to a serving dish. Remove and discard any herb stalks.

12. Ladle the stew into bowls and top each serving with a dollop of sour cream or crème Fraiche, if desired.

# *Greek*
# lamb pita
## *wraps*

Tzatziki recipe adapted from
*The 6-Week Cure for the
Middle-Aged Middle*,
Eades and Eades (Crown, 2010)

*Serves 4*
*Cooking time: 24 to 32 hours*

1. Fill and preheat the water oven to 134°F (56.5°C).

2. Put the lamb into a small (1 quart/.9 liter) food-grade cooking pouch and vacuum seal.

3. Submerge in the water bath and cook for 24 (or up to 32) hours.

*Make the Tzatziki Sauce*

1. Put all ingredients into the workbowl of a food processor or blender jar and process until smooth.

2. Taste and adjust seasonings, adding a bit more salt, pepper and/or vinegar to achieve a piquant flavor.

2 pounds (32 oz/.91 kg) boneless leg of lamb

1 teaspoon (5 ml) kosher salt

4 pieces pita bread

½ cup (2.5 oz/75 g) crumbled feta cheese

1 cup (3.7 oz/110 g) sun dried tomatoes packed in oil

½ cup (4 oz/118 g) kalamata olives finely chopped

1 bunch of scallions thinly sliced

*For the Tzatziki sauce*

½ medium cucumber, peeled, seeded, and chunked

½ cup (6 oz/170 g) plain yogurt, preferably Greek style

1 clove garlic, crushed

8-10 large fresh mint leaves

½ teaspoon (2.5 ml) coarse sea salt

¼ teaspoon freshly ground black pepper

¼ teaspoon (1.25 ml) onion powder

1 tablespoon (15 ml) red wine vinegar

3 tablespoons (45 ml) extra virgin olive oil (Greek if you've got it), divided use

Juice of ½ lemon

3. Pour into a container, cover tightly, and refrigerate for 30 minutes or longer to develop the flavors.

*Sear the lamb and assemble the wraps*

1. Remove lamb from water bath, pat dry, and season liberally with kosher salt.

2. Preheat a skillet over very high heat, and sear the lamb on all sides for 30 seconds to a minute.

3. Slice the meat thinly.

4. When ready to serve, heat the pita slices for 20 to 30 seconds in the microwave, or in a skillet, turning once.

5. Divide the lamb, feta, sundried tomatoes, kalamata olives, and scallions evenly among the pita pockets and finish with Tzatziki sauce.

# shepherd's pie

*Serves 4*

*Cooking time: 7.5 to 10 hours*

*Cook the meat*

1. Fill and preheat the water oven to 134°F (56.5°C) for medium-rare, 140°F (60°C) for medium.

2. Put the stew meat into a bowl, add the seasonings, and toss to coat the meat.

3. Heat the oil in a skillet over medium-high heat until shimmering.

4. Brown the meat on all sides in the hot oil. Remove from the skillet and allow the meat to cool.

5. Sprinkle the flour into the hot skillet and stir, allowing it to brown slightly.

*For the meat*

1 pound (16 oz/.45 kg) beef or lamb stew meat, cut into 1-inch (2.5 cm) cubes

1 teaspoon (5 ml) coarse salt

½ teaspoon (2.5 ml) black pepper

¼ teaspoon (1.25 ml) garlic powder

¼ teaspoon (1.25 ml) onion powder

2 tablespoons (30 ml) olive oil

2 tablespoons (30 ml) all-purpose flour

1 cup (8 fl oz/240 ml) beef broth

*For the vegetables*

1 small head cauliflower, washed and trimmed

2 tablespoons (60 ml) butter

salt and pepper to taste

10 to 12 pearl onions, peeled

2 carrots, peeled and cut into 2-inch (5 cm) pieces

*For the pie assembly*

Pouch of cooked cauliflower

¼ cup (2 fl oz/60 ml) heavy cream

6. Deglaze the skillet with the beef broth, stirring as the pan sauce thickens. Taste for seasonings and add a bit more salt or pepper to your taste, if desired.

7. Remove the sauce from the heat and allow it to cool.

8. Put the browned meat in a single layer into a large (1 gallon/3.8 liter) food-grade cooking pouch, and vacuum seal.

9. Submerge the meat fully in the water bath, and cook for 6 to 8 hours. At this point, you may continue with the recipe, or quick chill the pouch by submerging it in ice water for at least 30 minutes and refrigerate for up to 48 hours.

10. Pour the pan sauce into a zip-closure cooking pouch, use Archimedes' Principle (page 61) to evacuate the air from the pouch, and zip closed. (If using standard vacuum-seal pouches, press as much air as possible out of the pouch with your hands, and seal only. Do not attempt to vacuum seal liquids with a suction vacuum sealer.)

*Cook the vegetables*

1. Fill and preheat (or raise the temperature of) the water oven to 183°F (84°C).

2. Cut the cauliflower in half, then into ½-inch (1.3 cm) slices.

3. Put cauliflower into a large (1 gallon/3.8 liter) cooking pouch, along with the butter. Sprinkle with salt and pepper and vacuum seal the pouch.

4. Put the onions and the carrots into another cooking pouch, sprinkle with salt and pepper, and vacuum seal.

5. Put the pouches in the water oven and cook for at least and hour and up to 90 minutes. The vegetables must be submerged completely to ensure even cooking.

6. When the vegetables are cooked, reset the temperature in the water bath to 134°F (56.5°C). To speed the process along, remove 1 to 2 quarts/liters of hot water from the water bath with a large measuring cup and replace it with an equivalent amount of ice water.

7. When the temperature stabilizes at 134°F (56.5°C), return the meat and sauce pouches to the water bath, and let them come to temperature (about 30 minutes).

*Assemble the pie*

1. Preheat the broiler to high.

2. Remove the pouches from the water oven, open each pouch, and drain away the liquid from the pouches of meat and vegetables.

3. Pour the cooked cauliflower into the work bowl of a food processor or a blender jar, add ¼ cup (2 fl oz/60 ml) heavy cream and puree until smooth. Taste for seasonings and adjust with salt and pepper to your liking.

4. In a deep casserole dish, combine the meat, onions, carrots, and pan sauce and toss to coat evenly.

5. Top with the cauliflower purée, and spread it evenly over the pie.

6. Put the casserole under the broiler to lightly brown the top.

7. Serve immediately.

# measurements

Because of the precisely controlled temperatures used in sous vide cooking, recipes can be reproduced perfectly time after time. But as with any culinary technique, the success of the recipe also depends on correctly measured ingredients. Different ingredients are measured in different ways and, depending on where you live, using different measuring utensils. In order to ensure that our recipes can be successfully prepared by everyone—whether you live in Des Moines or Tokyo—the ingredient amounts have been specified using both volume and mass (weight).

Mass equivalencies for US volume measuring spoons (teaspoons and tablespoons) are given as UK metric measuring spoon (milliliters). (The same size measuring spoons in Asia are specified in grams.) The volume measure conversions based on cooking utensils are:  ¼ teaspoon = 1.25 ml spoon; ½ teaspoon = 2.5 ml spoon; 1 teaspoon = 5 ml spoon; 1 tablespoon = 15 ml spoon.

For liquids, a 1 cup measurement, as well as fractions of a cup, are converted to weights based on 8 fl oz being equivalent to 240 ml, the US FDA standard. Dry volume measures, as well as all other fluid measurements greater than 1 cup volume, have been converted to actual weights. For example, 1 cup of crumbled Feta cheese weighs 5 oz/150 g, while 1 cup of fine cornmeal weighs 6.3 oz/186 g. A pint of liquid is accurately converted to 16 fl oz/473 ml, not estimated based on 240 ml per cup. The accuracy of these conversions should make it simple to successfully produce the recipes worldwide.

The principle, first stated by Greek mathematician and physicist Archimedes, in the second century BCE, states: Any object, wholly or partially immersed in a fluid, is buoyed up by a force equal to the weight of the fluid displaced by the object. In sous vide cooking, we can use the principle to displace the air in a cooking pouch containing liquid. When we fill a pouch with food and liquid, because air is lighter than water, the weight of the water surrounding the pouch will force the residual air from the pouch, and then we can zip the pouch closed. Here are the simple steps:

1. Fill a zip-closure cooking pouch with food and fluid.

2. Lower the filled pouch, with the zip closure still open, into the water bath (or into a large pot of cooler water, if you prefer.)

3. The weight of the water in the bath or pot will press against the sides of the pouch and force the air out of the pouch as you lower the zip closure to the surface of the water.

4. Once the zip closure is at the surface and most of the air has been evacuated from the pouch, zip it closed.

5. The zip-sealed pouch should now stay submerged.

This principle can be used to evacuate most of the air from a cooking pouch containing liquid, which can be difficult to handle with a suction vacuum sealer. Using a zip-closure cooking pouch and Archimedes' Principle makes it easy to prepare sauces, syrups, glazes, infusions, ice cream bases, soups, stews, braises, and more in the sous vide water oven.

ISBN: 978-0-9844936-3-0

Printed in the United States of America.
First Edition
1 2 3 4 5 6 7 8 9 10

Book design by Faith Keating

**Paradox Press**